# Fun in the Sun

T0337094

Written by Jane Clarke

Illustrated by Leesh Li

**Collins**

# Who's in this story?

Listen and say

Mum

BUS

Download the audio at www.collins.co.uk/839786

Oz

Sara

Sara, Oz and Mum are on the bus.

4

They are at the beach.

Sara and Oz are in the sea.

This is fun!

6

Mum doesn't want to get water on her.

Sara! Oz!

7

Mum says, "Let's have ice cream."

A big bird wants Sara and Oz's ice creams!

No!

Oh no!

9

Mum says, "Make a sandcastle."

Mum doesn't like sand.

Sara and Oz are playing ball.

13

Mum says, "Let's have lunch."

Mum doesn't like sand
in her sandwiches.

Mum says, "Let's look in the rock pools."

Look at this beautiful shell.

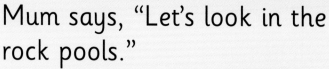

17

Mum says, "Let's go home."

18

Sara, Oz and Mum get the bus home.

It's fun at the beach in the sun.

# Picture dictionary

Listen and repeat

beach     ice cream     rock pool

sand     sandcastle

sandwich     sea     shell

# 1 Look and order the story

# 2 Listen and say

# Collins

Published by Collins
An imprint of HarperCollins*Publishers*
Westerhill Road
Bishopbriggs
Glasgow
G64 2QT

HarperCollins*Publishers*
1st Floor, Watermarque Building
Ringsend Road
Dublin 4
Ireland

William Collins' dream of knowledge for all began with the publication of his first book in 1819.

A self-educated mill worker, he not only enriched millions of lives, but also founded a flourishing publishing house. Today, staying true to this spirit, Collins books are packed with inspiration, innovation and practical expertise. They place you at the centre of a world of possibility and give you exactly what you need to explore it.

© HarperCollins*Publishers* Limited 2020

10 9 8 7 6 5 4 3 2

ISBN 978-0-00-839786-9

Collins® and COBUILD® are registered trademarks of HarperCollins*Publishers* Limited

www.collins.co.uk/elt

British Library Cataloguing in Publication Data

A catalogue record for this publication is available from the British Library.

Author: Jane Clarke
Illustrator: Leesh Li (Beehive)
Series editor: Rebecca Adlard
Commissioning editor: Fiona Undrill
Publishing manager: Lisa Todd
Product managers: Jennifer Hall and Caroline Green
In-house editor: Alma Puts Keren
Project manager: Emily Hooton
Editor: Tessie Papadopoulou-Dalton
Proofreaders: Natalie Murray and Michael Lamb
Cover designer: Kevin Robbins
Typesetter: 2Hoots Publishing Services Ltd
Audio produced by id audio, London
Reading guide author: Emma Wilkinson
Production controller: Rachel Weaver
Printed and bound by: GPS Group, Slovenia

Download the audio for this book and a reading guide for parents and teachers at www.collins.co.uk/839786